AND NOW, A WORD FROM OUR SPONSOR

The Story of a Roaring '20's Girl

Fran Parker

AND NOW, A WORD FROM OUR SPONSOR

The Story of a Roaring '20's Girl

BY DOROTHY AND THOMAS HOOBLER

AND CAREY-GREENBERG ASSOCIATES

PICTURES BY REBECCA LEER

SILVER BURDETT PRESS

Designed by Leslie Bauman

Illustrations on pages 51, 53, 54, 55, and 56
by Leslie Dunlap

Manufactured in the
United States of America

10 9 8 7 6 5 4 3 2 1

**Library of Congress Cataloging-
in-Publication Data**
Hoobler, Dorothy.
And now, a word from our sponsor :
the story of a roaring '20's girl /
by Dorothy and Thomas Hoobler
and Carey-Greenberg Associates
p.   cm.—(Her story)
Summary: In Overton, Ohio, in the 1920s,
Fran Parker and her family adjust to
such modern inventions as the radio and
the airplane, and Fran enters a radio contest.
[1. Family life—Fiction.   2. Radio
broadcasting—Fiction.   3. Contests—Fiction.
4. Airplanes—Fiction.]   I. Hoobler, Thomas.
II. Carey-Greenberg Associates.   III. Title   IV. Series.
PZ7.H76227An   1992
[Fic]—dc20   90-47815   CIP   AC
ISBN 0-382-24146-0 (lib. bdg.)
ISBN 0-382-24153-3

CONTENTS

CHAPTER ONE

"I Can Hear Music!"

"FRAN, CAN YOU come here a minute? I need your help."

Fran groaned. She had just flopped down on the front porch swing with a big glass of ice-cold lemonade. It was the first day of summer vacation. She didn't want to do anything but sit right here and watch the grass grow.

But in the Parker family it was almost impossible to do nothing for very long. The eight Parker children were always finding something new to work on.

From inside the big house came a loud squawk, followed by the sound of a piano played too fast. Eddie, one of Fran's younger brothers, was learning to play the trumpet. Henry, another brother, tried to encourage him by putting a roll of jazz music on the player piano. But Henry liked to pump the pedals as fast as he could, and the music came out tinkly and jumpy. It didn't matter, because Eddie could only make the trumpet sound like a sick cow.

"Fran!" And now Sam, Fran's oldest brother, was calling her from the side yard. Fran knew what he wanted. Last fall, Sam had bought a Model T Ford that had got stuck in a muddy road outside of town. The owner was disgusted with it and practically gave it away. Sam borrowed a horse to pull the automobile out of the mud and brought it home. Ever since then he had been trying to make it run.

"I know I've got it this time, Fran," Sam said. "But somebody has to sit in the driver's seat to control the spark while I crank it."

"That's what you always say," Fran said.

"I promise, you can drive it down to the corner if it starts."

Fran liked that idea. There were only about a dozen automobiles in their town, Overton, Ohio, in 1924. Most people still used horses and buggies. Actually, you could walk anywhere in town that you wanted to go. If you wanted to go anywhere else, you took the train that stopped in Overton twice a day.

Fran climbed up into the Model T. "My feet don't reach the pedals," she pointed out.

"That's all right," Sam said. "You just have to move this lever here. When you hear the engine catch, slide it down slowly. I'll jump in and do the rest."

Sam went around to the front of the car. He bent over to grab the metal crank that connected to the engine. "Ready?" he called.

"All set," said Fran.

Sam took hold of the crank with both hands. Fran had tried it once but couldn't move it at all. She could see it was hard for Sam too. Then the crank moved and Sam's head dropped out of sight.

Nothing happened. Sam's head bobbed up, then down again. He turned and turned.

Suddenly there was an explosion inside the engine. Smoke poured out. Fran moved the lever. Then came a series of loud bangs. She could feel the car shake. Sam was yelling at her, but she couldn't make out what he was saying. She pushed the lever all the way down. Now it sounded like somebody was inside the engine, hammering to get out.

Then the car gave a jump, and Fran grabbed the wheel. But the noises stopped, and so did the Ford.

Sam rushed around to the side of the car. His face was covered with soot. "Did you move the lever?" he yelled.

Fran nodded. Sam pounded his fist against the side of the car. "Shucks!" he said. "Nearly had it that time. Let's give it another try."

"Wait a minute," Fran said. "How safe is this thing?"

"Safe?" Sam looked like it was a new word to him.

"It sounded like it was going to blow up," Fran said.

"Oh, that's nothing," Sam said. "I've just got to make a few more adjustments." He opened the hood of the car and started to tinker inside.

Fran climbed down and watched him for a while. It looked to her like the engine needed more than adjustments. She went back to the porch.

The mail had come, and wouldn't you know? Nancy had grabbed both the porch swing and the new issue of *Vanity Fair*. Nancy was seventeen, and she wanted to be a flapper. There weren't any flappers in Overton, but there were lots of pictures of them in *Vanity Fair*. Father disapproved of them because they wore short skirts and used makeup. He wrote editorials about the flappers for the Overton *Weekly News*, which he owned and edited.

The only other magazine that had come in the mail was *Popular Mechanics*. Though it was Sam's magazine, Fran picked it up and began to look through it. Suddenly an article caught her eye: "How to Make Your Own Crystal Radio Receiver."

Nobody in Overton had a radio set. Fran knew, of course, that people in big cities could listen to music and plays broadcast over the air. But this article said that you could hear the programs even if you were hundreds of miles from the station.

Now this was exciting! The diagrams with the article were complicated, but Fran knew who could make sense of them. She went inside, where the boys were still making strange sounds, and started upstairs.

Fran shared a bedroom on the third floor with Olive, her twelve-year-old sister. Their parents had put them upstairs because Olive's passion was chemistry. Even before Fran got there, her nose told her that Olive was at work on another experiment. The door was closed, with a big sign saying DANGER! SCIENTIST AT WORK!

Fran ignored the sign and went in. Here the smell was almost overpowering. She ran to open a window. "Olive!" she said. "What's that smell?"

Olive looked up from her workbench. She pushed her long red hair back from her face. "Can you keep a secret?" she said.

"Olive, with the smell you're making, it's not going to be a secret for long."

"I hoped it would keep people away. I promised Nancy I'd try to make her some lip rouge."

Fran laughed. "If it smells like that, I don't think it's going to be very appealing. Anyway, Father won't let her wear lip rouge."

"Mother may change his mind," said Olive. "Nothing is impossible for the woman of today," she added. Olive often talked like that. She took after their mother, who had once led a march demanding the right of women to vote. Now Mother was a schoolteacher, but she also wrote a column for her husband's newspaper. Quite often her column opposed the editorials that Mr. Parker wrote.

"I had something else I thought you'd be interested in," said Fran. She held out the magazine. "This shows how to make a radio set."

Olive was interested. She took the magazine and lay down on her bed, where she liked to read. Fran sat down and looked at the picture of Madame Curie over Olive's bed. As Olive liked to point out, Madame Curie was the *only* person, man or woman, to win two Nobel prizes in science. Fran thought that Madame Curie probably didn't wear lip rouge, but she didn't mention that to Olive.

Olive read through the article quickly. She looked up when she was finished. "I like this," she said. "But there's a small problem. We need a crystal and earphones. The article tells where you can order them. But they cost three dollars."

Fran gulped. "That's a lot of money," she said.

Olive thought. "You can ask Father for it."

"Why me?" said Fran.

Olive stared at Fran, like an owl studying a mouse. "He's a bit concerned about you. You don't have any interests."

"I don't? I'm interested in a lot of things."

"But you haven't taken up a special project, like my chemistry, Sam's Model T, the boys' music lessons. Tell him you're interested in radio. He'll give in."

And that was the way it went. That evening the whole family gathered for dinner. As usual, Father asked each of his children what he or she was working on now. When Fran's turn came, she said, "I'm going to build a crystal radio."

Father's eyebrows went up. "Hmm," he said, glancing at Mother. "Ambitious project. But a bit useless. There's no radio station near us."

Fran swallowed and looked at Olive, who nodded. "I read an article that said you can hear stations even if they're hundreds of miles away. But I need three dollars for some parts."

"Well, that's a considerable sum." Father tugged his shirt cuffs down out of his jacket, the way he did when he was thinking. "I must say, I don't think much of this radio business. If you want to hear music, you can play the Victrola. Why listen to what someone else is playing hundreds of miles away when you can choose your own music?"

"They have lectures on the radio too," Olive put in. "And news. With radio, people don't have to wait for a paper to know what's going on."

Father's face got red.

That was the wrong thing to say, thought Fran. Father was proud of his newspaper. "It will never replace the printed word," he declared.

But then Mother spoke up. "You can't stop the wave of the future, dear," she commented.

"Humph!" Father snorted. "Not every new fad represents the future." He started to pull at his cuffs again but found that they were already down. He nodded at Fran. "If this interests you, I'll advance the money. But I expect to see a completed radio."

Fran smiled, and Olive gave her a thumbs-up.

Fran and Olive sent off the money the next day. While they waited for a reply, they gathered the other things they needed. Copper wire, a cardboard tube, and clips to hold the wires in place. "The chief thing is to have an antenna in a high spot," Olive said. "Our room is ideal."

Two weeks later, the earphones and crystal arrived. Fran brought the package upstairs, and the girls finished putting the radio together. Fran put the earphones on, and Olive attached the wires to the crystal.

Fran listened. "I can't hear anything."

"You have to keep moving the crystal," Olive explained. She fiddled with it some more.

"Wait. Keep it right there," Fran said. She strained her ears. Her face broke into a broad smile. "I can hear something, Olive. I can hear music!"

CHAPTER TWO

A Scoop

FRAN AND OLIVE found that the radio worked better at night. Pretty soon, they were pulling in stations from all over. Fran began to make a list of them: KDKA in Pittsburgh, WJZ and WEAF in New York, WGN in Chicago. Once they even heard WBZ in Boston. When a station opened in Columbus, Ohio, it came in clearly almost every night.

Everyone in the family took a turn at the earphones. Even Father. "Congratulations," he said. "You've succeeded. But the sound is so poor that I can't understand why you prefer this to the Victrola."

Father didn't feel the excitement of it, but

Fran did. Mother insisted that the girls turn out their light at nine o'clock, but Fran put on the earphones and lay in bed in the dark, listening. It was like traveling to these big cities that she had only read about. She could imagine the way the Starlight Ballroom in the Sheraton Hotel looked. And when Paul Whiteman's orchestra started to play, Fran could see the dancers in their tuxedos and gowns doing the fox-trot across the floor. She would fall asleep and dream of dancing with them all night long.

But something happened to turn Father into a radio "fan," which was a new word for fanatic. In July 1924, almost all the music programs stopped. The stations were broadcasting the Democratic Party presidential convention.

It started with a speech by William Jennings Bryan, who had run for president three times (but lost). Father insisted that everyone in the family listen. He even put the earphones on the twins, Victor and Violet, who were only five years old. "This is a chance to hear the greatest speaker of our time," Father said.

Fran admitted that Mr. Bryan was an exciting speaker, but she was glad she didn't have to listen to the whole speech. It lasted two hours. In fact, the convention was one of the most boring things she had ever heard. All the speeches were very long, but they turned out to be the good part.

The Democrats couldn't decide who they wanted to run for President. Each time they voted, every state announced who its delegates were for. It took almost an hour for one roll call of all the states. But nobody got enough votes. And so it went on day after day, night after night.

Amazingly, Father found this fascinating. He kept coming upstairs, only to find Olive busily mixing chemicals and Fran reading a book. "Aren't you listening?" he asked, and took up the earphones himself. He was very disappointed when Mother finally came up and insisted that the girls had to go to bed. It was impossible to move the radio because it was attached to the antenna.

"We could get a big set like the new one in the barber shop," Fran pointed out.

"Hmm, hmm," Father said, and Fran could see he was tempted. He tugged at his shirt cuffs, even though he wasn't wearing a coat over them. "Well, it would be a waste since the conventions are held only every four years."

But every night of the convention, Father came upstairs right after dinner. On the seventeenth night, he told the girls, "They're taking the one hundredth roll call of the states. Surely they'll decide now."

But they didn't, and Father kept the earphones on. It was a hot July night, and Olive and Fran went downstairs to the porch. Mother sat there fanning herself. The girls poured themselves glasses of lemonade.

"Mama, how long do you think this will go on?" Fran asked.

"The convention? As long as it has to. It's already the longest in American history."

"I'm tired of it," said Fran. "I wish the stations would play music again."

"Well, it's very important," said Mother. "The man they're choosing may be elected President."

"Perhaps they'll pick a woman," said Olive.

Mother chuckled. "You're right. But I'm afraid not this time. Women have only had the vote for four years. Though there are two women already running for state governors this year."

"There are?"

"Yes. In Texas and in Wyoming."

"Do you think they'll win?"

"If all the other women vote for them, they certainly will."

Just then, Father came out onto the porch. "It's over," he said. "One hundred and third ballot."

"Who won?" asked Mother.

"John W. Davis."

"I've never heard of him," Mother said.

They soon would hear a lot about Mr. Davis. Father was a loyal Democrat and wrote many editorials supporting Davis for President. But a lot of people in town favored President Coolidge, who was running for reelection as a Republican.

Mother surprised everybody. In her newspaper column, she announced that she favored Senator Robert M. LaFollette of Wisconsin. He was a member of a third party, the Progressives.

Her choice created a lot of heated arguments on the front porch after dinner. "LaFollette hasn't a chance," Father said. "His party is nothing but a collection of wild-eyed reformers."

"Well, then I am a wild-eyed reformer," Mother said. "LaFollette has the support of the farmers and the working people. Your Mr. Davis is a Wall Street banker. Coolidge has the support of big business. The rich will divide their votes among the two of them, and LaFollette will win."

All that summer it seemed like everyone was

talking about the election. Shopkeepers put pictures of their favorite candidate in the window. Fran noticed a lot of pictures of President Coolidge, but very few for John W. Davis or LaFollette.

On Labor Day, the Rotary Club held a big picnic on the village green. Practically everybody came. People displayed banners for their favorite candidates. The Coolidge people gave away little pins that said KEEP COOL WITH COOLIDGE. Davis's supporters had buttons too, but they just said DAVIS, with his picture. LaFollette couldn't afford metal pins; his backers gave away little paper folders with his picture.

Henry and Eddie collected all three, but Olive and Fran loyally wore only the LaFollette folders on their dresses. "The Coolidge people are giving away free hot dogs to anyone wearing a Coolidge pin," Eddie told them.

Fran was tempted, but Olive held her back. "Our votes aren't for sale," she said.

"We're not old enough to vote," Fran pointed out.

"What if Mother saw us?" Olive replied. That settled it. Anyway, Mother had packed a delicious meal of chicken, potato salad, and dilled beans. Afterward, the Rotary Club set up an ice-cream maker. It was hard work to churn cream in a barrel with dry ice packed around it, but after an hour, everybody got a scoop.

As Fran ate hers, she felt a little sad. The sun had set, and pretty soon everyone would go home. It was the end of summer, and tomorrow school would start again. She wouldn't be able to stay up late listening to the music from New York anymore.

But two months later she helped mother get another kind of scoop. November fourth was Election Day. A school holiday was declared so that the teachers could vote. Olive and Fran went with their mother to the courthouse. People were waiting in line in front of a booth with a curtain around it. When Mother's turn came, she went inside and marked her ballot. She came out with it folded in half and dropped it into a box.

As they left, Mother said, "That was the second time I've voted, and it felt just as good as the first time."

"Do you really think LaFollette can win?" Fran asked.

"Even if he doesn't," Mother said, "it is important to make your choice known. Whoever is elected will know that there are lots of people who support the Progressive cause."

"What about the women running for governor of Texas and Wyoming?"

"We probably won't know for several days. The newspaper comes out tomorrow, and it won't have the election results."

That gave Fran an idea. She set her alarm clock for 5:30. It was still dark when it went off, and Olive grumbled. But Fran put on the earphones and listened.

The first news was bad. Coolidge had won almost all the eastern states. He was sure to be re-elected President. LaFollette had won only his home state of Wisconsin.

But then the announcer said, "Here's a big surprise. We've just received a report that the nation has its first woman governor. Two of them, in fact. Nellie Ross of Wyoming and Miriam Ferguson of Texas were elected yesterday."

Fran jumped up and pounded Olive with a pillow. "They won!" she shouted.

The girls told their mother the news when she awakened. Mother hurried to her typewriter. "I'm going to write a new column with the news," she said.

When she finished, Fran and Olive ran to the printer's office with it. He was just starting to put the issue on the press, but he agreed to set Mother's new column in type and run it.

That afternoon Father came running up the steps to the house waving a copy of the newspaper. "Where did you learn this?" he asked Mother.

"Fran heard it on the radio this morning," she replied.

"Humph," he said. "I've been scooped in my own newspaper by my wife and children."

CHAPTER THREE

The Contest

TWO WEEKS LATER, a big wooden crate arrived at the Parkers' house. The children tried to peek inside to see what it was. Mother just smiled and said, "It's something your father ordered."

When Father came home, he and Sam took a crowbar and pried it open. The box held a big Westinghouse Aeriola Grand Radio! Inside the big mahogany cabinet were eight tubes that glowed when you turned the set on. Below was a big loudspeaker so that everybody could listen at the same time. "I suppose it *is* the wave of the future," Father said.

The new radio was much more powerful than the crystal one. At night the family could listen to all kinds of programs. One of Father's favorites was the Will Rogers show. Will Rogers was a cowboy who discovered that people liked the jokes he told. He started every program by saying, "I only know what I read in the newspapers." Then he went over the news of the day, adding his own funny comments. Father was delighted when Rogers imitated President Coolidge by making his voice sound dried-up and squeaky.

Henry and Eddie discovered that they could listen to football games each Saturday. Grantland Rice, the announcer, described each play so that you could see just what was happening. The roar of the crowd was almost as exciting, Fran thought, as hearing the music of the Starlight Ballroom.

There was still lots of music. Each program had its own musical group, and they were sometimes named after the sponsor of the program. Fran's favorite was a banjo band called the Cliquot Club Eskimos. Cliquot Club was a brand of ginger ale. The Parkers also listened to the A & P Gypsies, the Pure Oil Band, and the Firestone Orchestra.

Some programs were especially for children. At first, an announcer read aloud fairy tales and

other stories over the air. But soon, actors and actresses began to take the roles of the characters. And they could make sounds, like a creaking door, that made it seem as real as anything.

The sponsor of one of these programs was the Toasty Cereal Company. At the beginning and end of the program an announcer told how good Toasty Toasted Flakes were. Fran talked Mother into buying a box. It didn't taste as good as Fran thought it would, but Mother made her finish the box before she could have anything else for breakfast.

Still, the program was good. And one night, as Fran and Olive were listening, the announcer said the company was having a contest for children. The winner had to write fifty words or less on "The Most Important Invention of Our Time." The first prize was twenty-five dollars!

"I'm going to win that," said Olive. "I'll say the radio is the most important invention. The sponsors are sure to like that."

Fran was disappointed. She had that idea too. Olive said, "You can write about the same thing." But Fran knew that Olive's entry was bound to be better.

So Fran tried to think of something else. She asked Sam what he thought the most important invention of our time was. Naturally he said the automobile, but he was still making adjustments on his Model T. Fran decided she wouldn't choose that.

When Fran went to Nancy, she said the most important invention was obviously the movies. "How do you know?" asked Fran. "Overton doesn't even have a movie theater."

"But the movie stars are the most famous people in the world," Nancy said. "Charlie Chaplin, Mary Pickford, and Douglas Fairbanks are all millionaires. People all over the world love them because they're movie stars." Nancy sighed. "When I'm old enough, I'm going to Hollywood."

Fran wasn't satisfied with that either. She asked Father. "The electric light," he said. "It lets people work twice as long as they did before."

"Do they get paid twice as much?" Fran asked.

"Well, of course not. But they can get more done." That was a pretty good idea, but Fran wasn't quite sure it was right. She went to Mother.

"The right to vote will change the world more than anything else," Mother said. "It means there will be no more wars, for women won't allow it."

"I don't think that's really an invention," Fran said.

"It is a product of the human mind," Mother said. "Not all inventions are mechanical ones."

Maybe Mother's answer was best, but somehow Fran didn't think it fit the idea of the contest. She made a list of the ideas and looked through magazines to find anything else that was new. The vacuum cleaner, the fountain pen, the adding machine ... she even saw a picture of a gasoline-powered lawn mower. None of them seemed better than the radio.

The next day Fran came home from school and turned the radio on while she did her homework. She thought she might get some ideas for her essay. The news came on, and Fran heard that there was an epidemic of diphtheria in Nome, Alaska. Diphtheria was a serious illness and could spread rapidly. It was important for everybody in Nome to be vaccinated.

But there wasn't enough medicine there. "Nome is entirely cut off from the world at this time of year," the announcer said. "The Arctic Sea is frozen, and the nearest railroad is over six hundred miles away."

Fran went to the globe in the family library

and found Nome. It was way up on the northern coast. She shivered. Imagine how lonely it must be to live up there. What invention could help the people of Nome?

In the days that followed, everybody in the country heard about Nome on their radios. A short-wave station broadcast appeals for help. Finally, one brave man set out with a dog sled to try and reach Nome with the vaccine. Before he left, he told reporters that he had the best dog in the world—Balto. Through the crackle of static, Fran heard him claim, "Balto can get the vaccine through."

For a week nothing was heard from the man with the dog sled. The radio said that he was traveling through blinding snow with eighty-mile-per-hour winds, in temperatures that could fall to fifty below zero. Every day Fran came home from school and listened to the news bulletins.

At last, the news came: "We interrupt this program for a special bulletin. Gunnar Kasson and his dog, Balto, have reached Nome."

Balto became famous as the dog who saved Nome. All the newspapers printed pictures of him. A movie company offered Balto a contract, but his owner said Balto didn't like warm weather. "Imagine turning down a movie contract!" Nancy groaned.

"Is the dog sled a new invention?" Fran asked Sam.

"No, the Eskimos have used it for centuries," he said. "But you know what I think. They should have used an airplane."

"It couldn't have flown in a snowstorm," Olive said.

"Maybe not now. But someday, airplanes will be good enough to make that trip in a few hours, storm or not."

Fran jumped out of her chair. "That's it," she said. She went right upstairs and started to write. The first entry she wrote was over one hundred words. Too long. She cut it down, just the way Mother did to make her column fit in the newspaper. Finally she wrote:

"I think the most important invention of our time is the airplane. When I listen to the radio, I can imagine myself in faraway places. But with an airplane, I can actually go there, faster than anyone has ever traveled before. The airplane will make the world a smaller place."

The next morning she mailed it.

CHAPTER FOUR

"The Flapper"

MEANWHILE, the announcer kept on urging more people to enter the contest. He didn't say anything about when it would end. Every week Fran and Olive tuned in the program, waiting for them to announce a winner.

And wouldn't you know? Father discovered a new reason to dislike the radio. Sometimes, Fran thought, it was hard having a newspaper editor as your father. He was always looking for new ideas to write about, and somehow they turned out to be problems for you.

That winter it had snowed a lot in Overton. Walking home, Father decided that there were too few children out sledding or making snow-men. He decided that the radio was the reason. He wrote an editorial. "This device breeds lazi-ness," he wrote. "The children aren't interested in anything but lolling about listening to other people." He urged his readers to limit the amount of time the radio was played.

Of course, Father always took his own advice. At dinner that night he announced that the radio would not be played on Tuesdays and Thurs-days. "Oh no!" said Olive. "Tuesday is the night the Toasty Cereal program is on."

The girls begged Father to choose another night. But Will Rogers was on Wednesdays, and John Philip Sousa's band played on Mondays. These were Father's and Mother's favorite programs.

"We can provide our own entertainment," said Father. So on Tuesday night they listened to Eddie work the player piano. After half an hour of this, they thought Father would give up. But instead he said, "It wouldn't hurt any of us to read a good book."

The girls appealed to Mother. "Perhaps you should do something to show Father that you've learned from the radio," she suggested.

Fran and Olive talked it over in bed that night. "I know," Fran said. "We'll put on our own radio show."

"And we'll be the sponsors," said Olive. "Our message will be: Leave the radio on."

The next afternoon they worked together to write a script. They cast Nancy as the heroine. "She wants to go to Hollywood," Olive pointed out. "We'll let her practice."

Later they went over the script with Eddie and Henry. The four of them figured out how to make sound effects. They even worked in parts for the twins and Sam.

Thursday night, when the family was finishing dinner, Fran said, "We have a surprise planned." Father's eyebrows went up, and he said to Mother, "You see? The children are learning to entertain themselves."

"No, we want to entertain you," Fran said. "Wait a minute, and then come into the living room." The children left the table.

When they were ready, Father and Mother followed. They found all the lamps turned out except one behind the radio. Father and Mother sat on the couch.

"And now . . ." Fran said from behind the radio, "A Parker Family production. A radio drama entitled 'The Flapper.' " Eddie played dramatic music on the player piano.

Olive began to read the script. "Our heroine, Florence, yearns for stardom in the movies. But her father forbids it."

"Humph." This was Eddie, imitating Father. "No daughter of mine shall paint her face and bob her hair."

"Who's that supposed to be?" the real Father said. Fran saw Mother trying not to laugh.

"Go to your room," Eddie said, in Father's voice. Henry slammed the door to the kitchen.

Now Nancy, playing Florence: "I must go to Hollywood. My heart demands it. It is my destiny. I will bob my hair."

From behind the radio, Olive began to make clipping sounds with the scissors.

"I hope you're not really—" Father interrupted, but Mother shushed him. "They're only entertaining themselves," she said.

"And I will cut my skirt short, like a real flapper," said Nancy. More clipping.

Henry used a pair of Mother's shoes to make walking sounds on the floor. Nancy spoke, "Father, I have disobeyed you."

"Humph. Leave this house. You are no longer my daughter."

"Oh, that's not fair," the real Father said.

The door slammed again. Now the twins rattled a metal cooking sheet. "Thunder," said Nancy. "A storm is coming, and I have no place to go."

The twins began to drop dried peas into an empty can. One or two, and then handfuls of them.

"The storm is getting worse," Nancy said.

That was the cue for Fran's sound effect. She magnified her voice through a rolled-up tube. *"Whoo, whoo!"*

"A train," said Nancy. "*Chuff, chuff*," said Fran. Olive rang a bell. "The train is stopping," said Nancy. "It will take me to my new life."

More train noises followed. Then Fran said, in a deep voice, "Tickets please."

"I have no ticket," said Nancy.

"Leave the train."

"But it's moving too fast," said Nancy. "Please. Let me work for my ticket."

"You can wash dishes in the dining car," said Fran.

The twins clattered dishes together.

"Work faster," said Olive in her meanest voice. She slapped the back of her hand loudly.

On the sofa Father jumped. "Who did that?"

"Please don't hit me again," said Nancy. "I'm working as fast as I can."

Eddie played more music on the piano. They hadn't been able to think of anything else to happen to Florence on the train. Finally, Fran said, "All out for Hollywood!"

"I'm here at last," said Nancy. "Look at all the bright lights! The big houses! The fancy cars!" Eddie honked a horn with a big rubber bulb. They had borrowed it from the Model T. "Watch out or you'll get run over!" he hollered.

"I need a job," Nancy said. "There's a night-club. The sign says DANCERS WANTED."

"Humph!" said Father from the couch. Mother put her hand on his arm.

"Let me see you dance," said Henry.

The twins tapped shoes on the floor.

"You're hired," said Henry. "Get into this costume."

The piano began again. "What's that song?" asked Father. Fran and Olive giggled. They had borrowed a piano roll of the Charleston, a popu-lar new dance that Father would *never* have ap-proved.

Henry, as the nightclub owner, said, "That was good. A customer wants you to come to his table."

"Maybe this is a famous movie director," said Nancy.

Fran played the customer. "Sit down," she said, trying not to laugh. Eddie made a popping sound by pulling his finger out of his mouth. He loved doing that. "Have some champagne," said Fran.

Father cleared his throat.

"Oh no," said Nancy. "I promised my mother I would never taste strong drink." Father nodded firmly.

"Come on," said Fran gruffly. "You'll like it."

"Take your hand off my arm," said Nancy. She squealed. "Oh. You're hurting me."

Olive pounded her fist into a pillow as hard as she could. They had tried several things to make the sound of a punch. This worked best.

"Don't bother this girl again." This was Sam, who agreed to play the most important role.

"Thank you, sir," said Nancy. "Why . . . I recognize you."

"Yesss," said Sam.

"You're Rudolph Valentino. The movie star."

"Yesss. Would you like to be in my new movie?"

While Eddie played the piano, Olive read again: "And so Florence's dream came true. The next day she was trapped in a forest fire." The twins rolled cellophane between their hands. It really did sound like a fire.

"And then came the sound of hoof beats." Eddie and Henry rapped walnut shells against the floor.

"Valentino swept her into his arms . . ." continued Olive.

"Cut!" said Fran. "That's a great scene. You're going to be a big star, Florence."

"I have only one more wish," said Nancy.

Olive took over. "Nancy's, I mean, Florence's wish was to have the movie shown in her hometown, Overton, Ohio. And it was granted."

The twins turned on the vacuum cleaner.

"What's that?" Father said.

Olive and Fran answered at once. "An airplane," they cried. "What's an airplane doing in Overton?"

The twins turned the cleaner off, and it whirred to a stop. "Look who's getting out!" said Fran.

"It's our lost sister, Florence!" said Olive.

"Look! Isn't that Rudolph Valentino with her?"

"It is! It is!" shouted the twins.

"Run and tell Father," said Fran.

Eddie played music. "Father," said Nancy, "I

am a star now. The studio paid me ten thousand dollars. Now you won't have to work so hard."

"Humph!" said Eddie. "You've succeeded."

"Do you forgive me?"

"Yes. You can come home now. But no lip rouge."

Mother could not stop laughing. Even Father applauded.

"And now," said Fran. "A word from our sponsor."

She and Olive read the message they had prepared. The radio taught people many things about the world. "It is a means of education," Olive said.

"And so," added Fran, "we should be allowed to listen to our programs."

"Particularly since we have a serious interest in one," said Olive. "Fran and I have entered an essay contest, and it's nearly certain that one of us will win."

"Humph," said Father. He looked at Mother.

"You must admit," she said, "that tonight's entertainment was very creative."

"Oh, all right," said Father.

CHAPTER FIVE

The Barnstormer

IT WAS SPRING again, and through the bedroom window Fran could hear the birds singing. Though it was Saturday, she didn't want to get out of bed. She was wondering about the contest. It had been two months since she had mailed her entry, and still no winner had been announced on the radio. Maybe she should have written about something else.

Gradually, Fran became aware of another sound a long way off. It sounded a little like the vacuum cleaner. But as it grew louder, she realized it was more powerful than that.

Eddie and Sam were shouting below her window. Fran got up and looked out. Sam was pointing up in the sky. As she looked, an airplane flew overhead. She rubbed her eyes. Maybe she was dreaming. It was just like the radio play she had written.

Fran dressed quickly and went out. A lot of their neighbors were watching too. The airplane was swooping low over the town. It circled and came back, and then dipped below the trees. "It's going to land!" Eddie shouted. They all ran in the direction the plane had gone.

It had landed on the high-school baseball field. The pilot turned it around and taxied back toward the crowd. Fran saw that it was a two-seater, with a passenger in back of the pilot.

The man in the back climbed out of the plane. He was wearing a sharp-looking plaid suit. "Is this Overton, Ohio?" he shouted toward the crowd.

"Yes!" they yelled back. He walked toward them. "Can anyone tell me how to find a young girl named Fran Parker?"

Fran's heart stopped. This really must be a dream. But the others pushed her to the front of the crowd. "Here she is! This is her."

Fran's legs were wobbly. "You're Fran Parker?" the man said. She opened her mouth but couldn't say anything. Olive stepped up next to her. "She's Fran Parker. I'm her sister."

"Well, she writes better than she talks," he said with a grin. "I'm Hiram Jones, of the Toasty Cereal Company. I've come to Overton to award Fran the first prize in our essay contest."

Fran's brothers and sister clapped her on the back. Fran held onto Olive to keep from being knocked down. "Oh, Olive," Fran said. "I'm sorry you didn't win."

"Are you kidding?" said Olive. "You always have been a better writer than me."

"I didn't know you thought so," said Fran.

"Scientists are known for their poor writing ability," Olive explained.

"Since you wrote about the airplane," Mr. Jones said, "we thought we'd put on a flying exhibition right here in Overton." He waved to the pilot, and the plane's engine roared. It moved across the field faster and faster, and then rose into the sky.

The plane went up so high that they could barely see it. Then it turned and headed for the ground. People screamed, "He's going to crash!" But at the last minute the pilot leveled off, and the plane roared over the crowd. Everybody screamed and put their hands over their heads.

Then he went up in the sky and dived again. This time the plane did a loop, forming a circle just like an ice skater on a pond. Fran was fascinated. Even though she'd written about the airplane, she hadn't known how exciting it was to see one actually fly.

Next, the pilot turned the plane upside down and flew over the field. He waved at them with both hands. Everybody gasped. "How does he keep from falling out?" Fran asked.

"Oh, he's strapped into the seat," Mr. Jones said. "Don't worry. He's a barnstormer. Puts on this kind of show all over the country. Sometimes he even gets out and walks on the wing."

"Oh no!" said Fran.

"When we're up in the air, I feel as safe with him as if I was in church," Mr. Jones said. "How'd you like to take a ride?"

"*Me?*" Fran said. "Omigosh!"

"I'll take your picture," Mr. Jones said. "The Toasty Cereal Company would like to use it in an ad. That reminds me. Are your parents here?"

"No," said Fran. "They're at the newspaper office today. Father's the editor."

"Is that so?" said Mr. Jones. "Excellent. We'll go over and talk to him."

The plane landed, and the crowd applauded.

The pilot climbed down to the ground. He took off his leather helmet and goggles. He was a tall, thin young man with blond curly hair. Fran thought he was way more handsome than Rudolph Valentino.

"This is Charles," Mr. Jones said. He went with them to the newspaper office. Olive ran inside ahead of them. "Fran won!" she announced. "Fran won the contest, and they've brought an airplane to Overton!"

Father looked up from his big roll-top desk. He blinked. "Contest?" he said. Mother walked over from the other side of the room. "You remember, dear. The Toasty Cereal Contest. That's wonderful news!"

Mr. Jones explained that they would like to give Fran a ride in the airplane. Father tugged at his cuffs and looked at Charles. "You're the pilot? What's your name?"

"Charles Lindbergh, sir. Your daughter will be safe with me. I haven't lost a passenger yet."

"Humph." Father looked at Mother. Mother said, "Fran? Would you like that?"

"Oh, I would. Yes," Fran said.

"Well, then you shall."

Mother and Father went back to the baseball field with them. By now a bigger crowd had gathered to admire the plane. Charles, the pilot, made sure Fran was strapped into her seat securely.

Fran was starting to feel nervous by now. It was fun to watch the plane, but realizing she was actually going to fly was something else. But it was too late to say no. Charles started the engine by turning the propeller, and then climbed aboard. The engine roared, and off they went.

Just moving along the ground was pretty exciting. Fran waved to her family as the plane rushed past them. She could feel the wheels rolling along the ground, and then . . . nothing. The plane lifted into the air. She was flying!

They rose quickly above the trees beyond the field. Fran peeped over the side and watched the ground get farther and farther away. All at once she wasn't frightened any more.

It was so thrilling! She could see all of Overton like a doll village below her. But now she began to look around her and realized that the most exciting thing was actually being in the air. The wind rushed past her face, and she knew what it meant to be "free as a bird."

All those nights listening to the radio, she had imagined traveling to be with people in faraway places. Now she was part of the air, like the mu-

sic and voices that came over the radio. She had the feeling she could go anywhere, be anything she wanted. Fly with the wind. Free.

Charles looked over his shoulder at her. He made a little circle in the air with his finger. He was asking if she wanted to do a loop! Without thinking, she nodded yes. She held tightly onto the sides of the plane, and they swooped up and over. Fran was sure she screamed, but the engine was so loud she couldn't hear herself.

Olive told her later they were only in the air about ten minutes, but it seemed like hours. Even then, Fran was disappointed when she saw the plane headed toward the field again. Everybody rushed forward as the plane touched down, and she saw Mr. Jones taking pictures with his camera.

When Fran finally got out, her legs were rubbery. "Hard getting used to the ground again, isn't it?" said Charles.

"I wished we could stay up forever," Fran said.

He smiled. "I feel the same way myself."

Mother invited Charles and Mr. Jones to have lunch with them, and they all went back to the house. As they turned up the walk, Charles saw the Model T standing in the yard. "Looks like somebody's working on a car," he said.

Sam admitted it was his. "Haven't been able to get it running," he said.

"Let's have a look," said Charles.

Wouldn't you know, before lunch was ready, he had done something to the engine that made it run. They all climbed in, and Sam beamed with pride as he drove it around the block.

At lunch everybody wanted to ask Charles questions. Fran was annoyed, because she wanted to talk to him herself. He winked at her, and she blurted out, "Can women fly planes too?"

"Why sure," he said. "A young woman named Amelia Earhart is a terrific flyer."

"I'm going to do that too," Fran said. Father looked at Mother. "You never know," Mother said.

"I read your contest entry," Charles said. "I liked it. There's a contest that I'm going to try to win someday."

"What's that?"

"People have offered twenty-five thousand dollars for the first pilot to fly across the Atlantic. When I get better at flying, I'm going to do it if nobody else has."

"Across the Atlantic!" Fran gasped. Everybody else was listening now.

"How long would it take?" Olive asked.

"I figure about thirty hours or so."

"Wouldn't you fall asleep?"

Charles looked at Fran. "Did you feel like falling asleep when you were up there?"

"Oh no," said Fran. He smiled and nodded.

They went back to the field to see Charles and Mr. Jones off. As the plane rose into the air, Charles looked back and waved at Fran. She watched till the plane was just a speck in the sky. "Someday," she said.

Two years later, the whole country was glued to the radio for a day and a half. It was just like the story of Balto. But Fran and her family were more excited than anyone else. The radio had announced that Charles Lindbergh had taken off from Long Island to fly to Paris.

For more than a day nobody heard from him. Then the radio said his plane had been seen over Ireland. Fran ran onto the lawn, shouting for everybody to hear, "He made it!"

A few hours later, Lindbergh landed in Paris and became the most famous man in the world. Fran wrote Mother's column in the paper that week, telling about her flight with Lindbergh. Father read what she wrote and nodded. "You'll run this paper someday," he said.

Fran smiled. She was thinking about the sky.

MAKING YOUR OWN RADIO

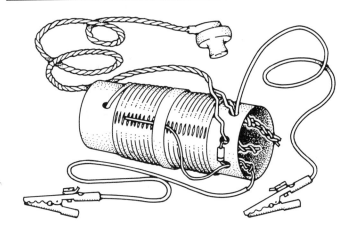

IN THE EARLY days of radio, many people made their own crystal radio receivers, just as Fran and Olive did in the story. No power source was needed, for the radio station's signal was (and is) powerful enough to be picked up by a simple receiving set. When the family got their larger Westinghouse set, with a loud-speaker, it was powered by large batteries. Radios that could be plugged into house electric wires came later. Vacuum tubes were used to make the signal stronger and louder. Then, in the late 1940s, tiny transistors began to replace the large vacuum tubes.

You can make your own radio receiver in about an hour, using a transistor instead of a crystal. The transistor you can use is called a germanium diode (jer-MAY-nee-um DYE-ohd.) You can buy one for about a dime at any electronics hobby store. You will need an earphone. Simple ones cost about a dollar. You will also need about 35 feet of thin, insulated wire, but this too is inexpensive and easy to find. The only tools you need are a wire-stripper (a small scissors will do) and possibly a screwdriver, if you use the alligator clips shown on the previous page.

There is no danger of electric shock, because you won't even need batteries. (Of course, don't try poking any of your radio's wires into an electrical socket!)

Use the diagrams to follow the directions, and the job will be easy.

Materials Needed

Cardboard tube, like the inside of a paper towel roll, Rubber band (a wide one is best), Germanium diode, Earphone with wire leads, 35 feet (11 meters) of No. 22 gauge insulated wire,

Coarse sandpaper, Hole-puncher (a sharp-pointed scissors will do), Wire-stripper (or scissors), Two alligator clips (not absolutely necessary), Screwdriver (not absolutely necessary).

Steps

1. Use your hole-puncher to make three small holes in the cardboard tube. The holes should be about an inch apart, and close to the end of the tube. (See diagram below, where the holes are numbered 1, 2, and 3.) When the directions below tell you to put wires into these holes, poke the wire from the outside of the tube into the inside—*except* in Step 14.

2. Cut off about six feet (two meters) of the wire and set it aside for later.

3. Take the rest of the wire, and strip off about one inch of insulation from one end.

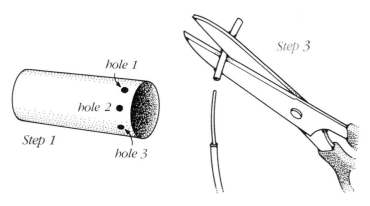

hole 1

hole 2 ●

Step 1

hole 3

Step 3

4. Poke the bare end of this wire through hole #1.

5. Carefully wind the rest of the long wire around the cardboard tube. Don't overlap the wire, but keep the coils next to each other. (See diagram.)

6. If you want, you can make another hole in the tube where the wire ends. Tuck the end inside to keep it out of the way. It won't be attached to anything.

7. Use the sandpaper to sand off a strip of insulation along the wire coils wrapped around the tube. Keep sanding until you can see the silver or copper wire under the insulation. It's better to sand too much off than not enough. (See diagram.)

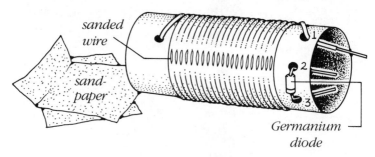

8. Now put your germanium diode in place. Each end has a wire attached to it. Tuck one into Hole 2, and the other into Hole 3. Bend them to keep them in place. (See Tips.)

9. Take the six feet of wire you set aside earlier. Cut it in half, making two three-foot sections. (Wire A and Wire B)

10. Strip about an inch of insulation off both ends of Wire A. For Wire B, strip one inch of insulation off one end, and six inches off the other end.

11. Take Wire A and poke one end through Hole 1. You should now have two wires through this hole.

12. Strip an inch of insulation off the ends of the two wires attached to your earphone. Poke one wire through Hole 1. Twist the bare ends of all three wires in this hole together.

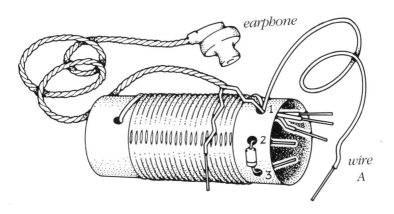

13. Poke the other earphone wire through Hole 2. Twist the bare wire around the diode wire that is already in this hole.

14. Now take the *long* stripped end of Wire B. Put it *inside* the tube and tuck it *out* through Hole 3. Leave a little bit of bare wire inside the tube, and twist the diode wire around it.

15. Make a loop with the bare end of Wire B. Use the rubber band to attach the end to the tube, where you have sanded off the insulation. (See diagram.) The rubber band should be tight enough to hold Wire B against the coil, but loose enough so that you can move it up and down the tube.

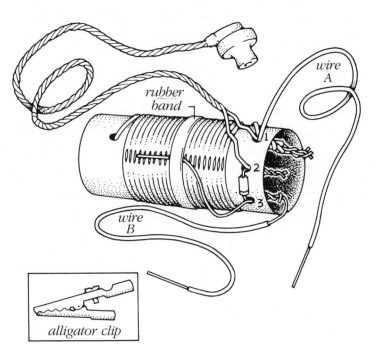

wire A

rubber band

wire B

alligator clip

16. The bare ends of Wire A and Wire B outside the tube can be attached to alligator clips with a screwdriver. This only makes it easier to attach them to an antenna and a "ground." If you like, you can simply twist the bare ends around an antenna and "ground."

Using the Radio

Attach either Wire A or Wire B to a faucet, copper pipe underneath a sink, or a metal radiator. This is your "ground." The other wire can be attached to an antenna. The better antenna you have, the more stations your radio will receive. Just by holding the bare wire end between your fingers, you can make your body into an antenna. A long wire hung out an upstairs window can be another antenna. If you have a dial telephone, the metal finger-stop will make a good antenna, because it connects to the telephone wires.

When you have the antenna hooked up, put the earphone in your ear. Then move the end of Wire B slowly across the sanded part of the coiled wire on the tube. When you hear a station, use the rubber band to keep your "tuner" in place.

Tips

Just as Fran and Olive found out, your radio will probably work better at night. Also, the closer you are to a radio station, the better your signal will be. You will also find that weather conditions affect your reception. Experiment at different times.

Your germanium diode may have a band painted on one end. If so, attach the painted end to Wire B (Hole 3) and the other end to the earphone wire (Hole 2).

It may take a little practice to strip insulation from the wires without cutting the metal wire underneath. You may find a wire-stripping tool around the house. Or, take a small scissors and cut the insulation all around the wire. You should then be able to pull off the insulation with your fingers. When you cut off the six inches of insulation from Wire B, it may be easier to do a little at a time.

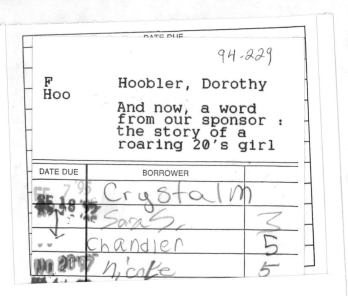

94-229

F
Hoo

Hoobler, Dorothy

And now, a word
from our sponsor :
the story of a
roaring 20's girl

DATE DUE	BORROWER	
SE 7 95	Crystal M	
	Sara S.	3
	Chandler	5
NO 20	nicole	5

F
Hoo

Hoobler, Dorothy

And now, a word
from our sponsor :
the story of a
roaring 20's girl